Other Titles by TW Brown

The DEAD Series

The New DEAD series

Zomblog

That Ghoul Ava

Loved to Death

TW Brown

Printed in the U.S.A.

ISBN 978-1-940734-72-9

Todd TW Brown left us way too soon on June 10th 2020 at the age of 54. He was always writing. Always thinking of new stories to tell. I found a few and thought you would like to see some more of his works.

RIP Todd. I will miss you!
9/18/1965 to 6/10/2020

Acknowledgements

I want to thank everyone that has read Todd's books for bringing him the joy of his life. He was always a writer. If he didn't write it would build up and come out in different ways. He had a dream and persued it. He wanted to share his stories with everyone. I am happy that he got the chance to fulfil his dreams.

Todd was one of the most amazing people I ever had the chance to meet. My world was better because he was in it. The 19 years I spent with him was simply not enough.

Through his stories, he will live on forever. I hope you enjoy them as much as he did writing them

Denise Brown
2020

Loved To Death

Sitting on the floor in a puddle of blood, my mind raced through the nightmarish whirlwind of events that led me to this heinous conclusion. Looking at the body sprawled across my legs; I tried to recall how things managed to fall apart so swiftly. The theme one of those television tabloid shows echoed in my head, and I could almost imagine seeing myself being led from some courtroom, coat tossed over my head to hide my identity. What good did that really do? They always managed to dig up some old dog-eared photo anyway.

The body twitched once, startling me back to reality. A jolt of electricity coursed through my veins...reality! I was now a murderer. That is about as real as it gets. How does one go about placing that on a resume so that it does not sound so sinister? I am really quite a nice guy. Just ask anybody. Well, anybody except my wife that is.

The easiest thing I could do now would be to put a gun in my mouth and pull the trigger. The only flaw in that plan is that I don't own a gun. Sure, there are other ways to commit suicide, none of which I would be willing to consider at this moment. "What the hell have I done?" my own voice caused me to jump. A slight chuckle that unsettled me echoed in the otherwise silent room. I looked around for a moment until I realized that I was the source of the peculiar laugh. So this is what happens when you start to lose your mind. How did I come to this point? Well, if you have a minute, I'll share my story with you. I guess I should go back a few days, when I was just a normal guy working a boring nine to job. Every day I woke up at around seven, and got home by six that evening. My wife, let me rephrase that, late wife, would usually leave and get home around the same time.

We usually made dinner together, ate, watched some television, and went to bed. Some nights we had six, other nights we didn't. As you can see, a pretty normal and routine life just like yours I'll bet. It has been the same for the six plus years we have been married give or take a slight variation every once in a while. Last night, a big wrench threw the gears off my daily routine. During dinner, my wife looks to me and says, "We need to talk." That alone was nothing to toss my life down the black hole it seems to be resting in now, it was the next sentence.

"I want a divorce."

I guess I sat there a while in silence. I really don't recall how long though. Finally, my brain kicked my mouth into gear, "What?"

"I said I want a divorce," she repeated.

"Ummm," not my brightest moment, but hey, I was dumbfounded. "Can I ask why?"

"I'm just not happy," she actually shrugged her shoulders. Can you believe that? Here she was asking for a divorce and she shrugs her shoulders like she is choosing between one repeat on television versus another.

"Is it something I've done'?" I asked. I must admit that I really had nothing more provoking than that to ask at first. It was like I was suddenly struck by idiocy. Here was my wife of six plus years asking for a divorce out of the blue and the best I could do was the old standard 'is it me?' line.

"Not really," my wife shrugged again. Maybe it was just me, but that little gesture started to really piss me off! I mean really now, how detached could this woman be to the man she made vows of 'till death do us part' with? "It's just that this relationship has run its course."

Run its course? What in the world did she mean by that? An idea sprang to my head. "Is it somebody else?" I asked, not really wanting to know the answer to that question. But at least I would have a better reason than the one she currently stood on.

"You should know me better than that," my wife snapped at me. Yeah, I thought, that's why this divorce request has caught me totally by surprise.

"I thought so too until about two minutes ago," I quipped somewhat harshly. Now that was a bit more witty my mind applauded.

"There is no need to get nasty," my wife glared. That was the first straw to cause the camel's back to begin its slow break.

"I'm sorry," I shot back. The rapier that is my wit gleamed somewhat brighter. "I guess I should be breaking out our best wine and some fine crystal goblets to celebrate this milestone in our illustrious marriage." Touché.

The rest of the conversation was more or less a verbal sparring match. When it was over, we went to bed. Let me clarify that...she went to bed. I slept on the couch. Perhaps I should clarify that as well. I curled up on the couch and stared at the blank television screen until I heard the alarm clock go off in what used to be our bedroom.

I went through all my usual routines that preceded my departure from work. I deliberately let my wife leave first then I called in sick. After that I walked down to my car and set on what I imagined would be a personal voyage of discovery. In other words, I drove to where my wife worked. I guess I was surprised to see her car parked in the front of the office complex that she worked in.

Finding what I considered to be a good spot for surveillance, I commenced my stake-out. Turning on my radio, I made a discovery over the next few hours. Every love song describes your exact feelings about your spouse or significant other. I eventually found a talk station. Just my luck, some damned relationship counselor spewing useless crap about love, marriage, and relationships.

The lunch hour came and finally a reward for my time. My wife emerged from her office, and with a strange man! No reason eh? I watched as she climbed into this man's car and the two drove off. Remembering everything I ever learned from the large quantities of cop shows on television, I slipped in a few cars back and followed.

I was not surprised in the least when the car turned into a hotel. My stomach began to churn as I watched my wife and that strange man walk into the hotel. Through the glass doors I could see them approach the front desk. Within moments they were handed a key and the two disappeared into the depths of their little love nest.

I parked the car and entered the main lobby. I quickly spied my wife and her secret lover standing at an elevator. Doing my best to remain inconspicuous, I waited until they entered the elevator then rushed over to see which floor they stopped at. The digital paned tipped me off to the fourth floor. I pressed the button to summon the elevator and waited for what seemed like days. The doors finally opened and I stepped in and hastily pressed the number four. Another eternity seemed to pass until I reached my destination. Stepping out into the hallway, I looked both directions. The hall was empty so I decided to just listen in at each door. Perhaps I would hear her voice in one of the rooms. Then what? Should I knock on the door? Perhaps go for the more dramatic and kick it in. I decided that I would make that decision once I found her.

It didn't take long. From inside one of the rooms I could hear the distinct sound of her laugh. It sounded so genuine, something I hadn't heard around the house in weeks, maybe even months. Was she really that unhappy being with me? I slumped against the door and received quite a surprise as the door fell open. I tumbled into the room and landed quite awkwardly on the floor. Looking up, I expected to find my wife and the strange man in the act of undressing. Imagine how stupid I felt when I looked up to see that the room was empty of furniture except for a long table. Sitting at the table was my wife...along with several other people!

This was no secret love nest! It was some sort of conference type meeting. Everybody had briefcases and all types of official looking folders open in front of them. I hurriedly scrambled to my feet and scrambled out the door putting it closed behind me. I ran down the hallway to the elevator and furiously pressed the button over and over in a vain attempt to make the doors open faster. I could hear the door opening back up the hall just as the elevator doors slid apart mercifully. Stepping in I pressed the lobby button.

Reaching the lobby I ran to my car and drove home. I could feel my heart just about ready to burst through my chest. I must have been home for over an hour before it finally began to slow down to a normal pace. The rest of the day, I felt like an inmate on death row waiting for the executioner to take me to the chair. Six o' clock came and went, followed by seven, eight, and nine. Maybe she wasn't coming home. Maybe she was so mad that she decided to stay at the hotel for the night in an actual room. I guess I couldn't really blame her. She must have been terribly embarrassed by my unannounced arrival.

I dozed off on the couch to the drone of the television. When I awake, it was to the sound of keys rattling the door. I closed my eyes hoping that she would think I was asleep. To my relief, it seemed to work because my wife closed the door and went directly to her room.

Opening my eyes just enough, I looked over at the clock on my VCR. It was after three in the morning! What the heck was going on here? I decided that I was going to out. I walked to the bedroom door and throw it open.

"You mind telling me where you've been?" I blurted out.

"Soon as you tell me what you were doing following me today," my wife snapped back. "I've never been so embarrassed in my life!"

"Don't go changing the subject," I shook my head. "I'll answer you after you tell me where you've been."

"it's none of your business, but if you really must know I went to a bar and had a few drinks." "Since when do you go out to bars on a work night?" I challenged.

That is exactly why I am leaving," my wife laughed. "We never do anything out of the normal routine. Everyday it's the same thing. We get up, go to work, come home, eat dinner, and then go to bed. When is the last time we did something spontaneous?"

"You never said anything," I whispered. "All of a sudden you just ask for a divorce. Not once did you ask me to do something different. Why can't we try that now? Why do we just have to get a divorce without even trying?"

"Because I don't love you anymore," she shrugged her shoulders again. That may have been what did it now that I think back.

"We took marriage vows for life," I could hear my voice starting to tremble. "Till death do us part and all that. Do you remember our wedding and vows we made?"

"Look," my wife began to usher me to the door, "I'm tired and this is really just a waste of time." "A waste of time!" now my blood began to boil. "You call trying to save our marriage a waste of time?" I stormed out of the room. I ñ stood there one more second, I was going to do something I have never done in my life, hit a woman. I flopped down on the couch and stared up at the ceiling. This seems to be the point where I lost track of time. I just lie there thinking of the vows we made. For some reason my mind kept going back to the 'till death do us part' line.

I really couldn't tell you how long I lay on that couch. I can't really tell you what happened other than this. I felt my body sit up. I stood and walked into the kitchen. I rummaged through a drawer and pulled out a big knife that I can't recall ever having used for anything since we bought the set it came with. I walked back to the couch and sat down again for a minute.

Till death do us part.

I stared at the blade as it caught the light from the television. We made vows for life. Now, she was just going to throw it away. After all the time we spent together there was just no way I could let it go.

Till death do us part.

I got up slowly, not really aware that I was walking to the bedroom. I opened the door and stood there for a moment. I could see the mound in the blankets that was my wife. I may have stood there for a minute or an hour. I really don't know how long. Eventually my feet started forward again as if on their own.

Till death do us part.

I felt my arm rise up and come down. The knife disappeared into the blankets and into my wife. I think she probably screamed, but I never heard her. My arm seemed to have its own mind as it rose and fell. At some point I guess she crawled out of the bed and into the hall.

So here I sit with absolutely no idea what to do. At least I can say that she lived up to her end of the vows. Wait a second, somebody is at the door.

I'm back now. I guess somebody heard the commotion because it is the police. They say I have to go with them. Thanks for taking the time to listen to my story.

MAY DECEMBER
Publications

**The growing voice in horror
and speculative fiction.**

Find us at www.maydecemberpublications.com
Or
Email us at twbrown.maydecpub@gmail.com

TW Brown is the author of the Zomblog series, his horror comedy romp, That Ghoul Ava, and, of course, the DEAD series and the New DEAD series. Safely tucked away in the beautiful Pacific Northwest, he moves away from his desk only at the urging of his Frisbee catching Border Collie Tyrion, or one of his Newfoundlands, Freyja or her younger sister Loki.

He plays a little guitar on the side...just for fun...and makes up any excuse to either go check on his beehives or strolling along his favorite place...Cannon Beach. His hobbies include training his Newfoundlands to be show dogs working on their championships, water rescue working on their WD titles and draft carts working on their DD titles. And we should never forget to add his African Greys named Sheldon, Lisa, and Paul. He answers all his emails sent to twbrown.maydecpub@gmail.com and tries to thank everybody personally when they take the time to leave a review of one of his works.

He can be found at www.authortwbrown.com. The best way to find everything he has out is to start at his Author Page. You can follow him on twitter @authortwbrown and on Facebook under Author TW Brown, and also under May December Publications.